For my own quirky turkeys.
I love you and I like you.

www.mascotbooks.com

Garbo and the Case of the Wet Footprints

For more information, please contact:
Mascot Books
620 Herndon Parkway, Suite 320
Herndon, VA 20170
info@mascotbooks.com

Library of Congress Control Number: 2020910325

CPSIA Code: PRT1020A
ISBN-13: 978-1-64307-392-7

Printed in the United States

GARBO
and the Case of the Wet Footprints

Gretchen Cleveland
Illustrated by Walter Policelli

"**Hullo, my name is Garbo.** I like marshmallows and mysteries. What do you know about these wet footprints?"

"Uhh, no-nothing," stammered the boy.

"Tut, tut," twittered Garbo. "What is your name?"

"Jonah," the boy said curiously.

"Well, Jonah," Garbo said, "surely you must know something! These wet footprints were not here all day, I presume?"

"Well, I guess not..." Jonah hesitated, retreating back to his front door. "I came home from school about half an hour ago, and I didn't see them."

"Aha! You do know something about these prints!" Garbo said, spotting Jonah's observation. "Come with me, my boy! This looks to be a five-mallow mystery!" Garbo said eagerly, tugging at Jonah. Jonah quickly grabbed his skateboard from behind the door.

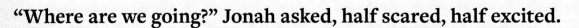

"Where are we going?" Jonah asked, half scared, half excited.

"To solve the case of the wet footprints, of course!" declared Garbo, fluttering down the street after the footprints with Jonah close behind. "I was out for a sunny stroll today when I came upon those curious footprints and I must simply find where they came from!"

Garbo stopped quickly and stared at the ground near his feet. "See here, Jonah?"

"I see sidewalk and grass," Jonah replied, gasping for breath. *Who knew turkeys were so fast?* he thought to himself.

"Yes, and what more, dear Jonah?"

"Oh! The footprints stopped?"

"Bingo!" shouted Garbo. "And what can you deduce from that?"

"If the footprints suddenly stopped, I guess whoever made them either flew off or ran into the grass..."

"Yes, Jonah!" exclaimed Garbo as he examined the grass.

"Wait, what are we looking for?" Jonah asked, sheepishly.

"Well what do you think we might find if the print-maker ran into the grass?"

"Maybe some smooshed grass, like that patch over there? Which must mean the feet went that way!" pointed Jonah, excited to finally be getting the hang of detective work.

"Yes! I think you have solved part of this mystery! Let us celebrate with a marshmallow," offered Garbo.

In the odd excitement of meeting a talking turkey and attempting to solve a mystery, Jonah hadn't seen that Garbo was carrying a skinny stick skewered with five fat marshmallows.

Garbo plucked a marshmallow from his thinking stick, divided it in half, and pondered the next step in the case while chewing his piece. Jonah devoured his immediately.

"Jonah, what do you think we should do now?"

"Follow the feet!" Jonah exclaimed.

"You lead the way!"

"Oh..." Jonah trailed off, stumped. "But how can we follow the footprints in the grass? They're so hard to see and I can't find any more than this patch."

"I am afraid we are at a juncture in this mystery at which we must apply our thinking caps," responded Garbo, pulling a top hat out of his back pocket. "When I do not know what to do next, I pretend I am enjoying a most delicious marshmallow from my thinking stick so that I cannot talk and must think instead."

After a long pause, Garbo said, "What if we considered what might have created the footprints?"

"Well these footprints are **GINORMOUS!**" said Jonah. "What in the world could have made them?"

"I do not have the slightest clue, but I suspect that such a large creature could not fly! Since we do not see any other smooshed grass, I anticipate the critter likely climbed itself that-a-way," replied Garbo, pointing to a large locust tree a few feet away.

At that very moment, Jonah looked up into the locust to find the shaggiest, whitest beast he'd ever seen—and it was crying. Jonah scrunched his face in wonder. "Garbo, what do we do?" he whispered.

"Tut, tut, there is only one thing TO do!" cried Garbo. "We must ask this crying Yeti if she would like some help!" With that, Garbo walked toward the Yeti.

"A YETI?!" screeched Jonah. "Everyone told me they were pretend, but I always knew they were real!"

"Sometimes believing does not require seeing, sweet Jonah." Garbo smiled. "Let us commemorate our detective work with another luscious marshmallow!" Garbo split the second marshmallow with Jonah.

Once finished, Garbo and Jonah approached the locust tree and the Yeti valiantly tried to shrink herself. It didn't work. Garbo pointed his beak up toward the sky, now at the base of the tree, and very gently asked, **"Dear Yeti, why are you crying?"**

Not surprisingly, the Yeti didn't speak; she simply clung to the branches, peering down at the crazy talking turkey and young boy.

Seeing that the Yeti was afraid, Jonah took a turn and asked, "Yeti, can we please help you with something?"

The Yeti started to warm up to the quirky duo, who seemed to be kind. She pointed to the tree and signed "more." Then she put her hand over her eyebrows and moved her massive head from side to side, as if she was looking for something from her perch in the leaves.

"She's looking for leaves? Or twigs? That doesn't make sense..." Jonah said.

"I am not sure what she is looking for. Let us again apply our thinking caps," replied Garbo. He closed his eyes, his beak still pointed to the sky.

Garbo opened his eyes quickly. "What do you suspect Miss Yeti was doing with her hands?"

"I don't know—I'm not a Yeti expert," laughed Jonah. "What does your thinking cap tell you?"

"My cap tells me that she must be using a special code to communicate and that the secret to this mystery is hidden in her hands."

Jonah scrunched his face again. This wild turkey wasn't making any sense.

"Let me ask her again, maybe that will help," said Jonah. He looked up at the tree. The Yeti looked even sadder than when they found her crying. "Yeti, can you please repeat what you just told us?"

Garbo and Jonah watched intently as the Yeti signed "more," then looked around the sky. Jonah's mind raced.

"I know, I know!" Jonah shouted. **"She's looking for more trees—she's lost! We need to help her find her way home!"**

Listening from above, the Yeti nodded excitedly.

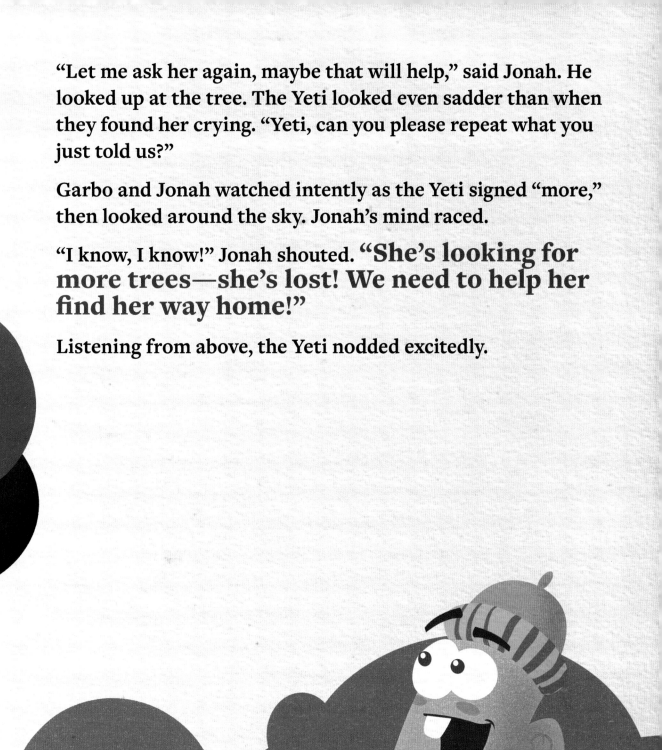

"**Congratulations, my dear boy!** By the looks of Miss Yeti's response, you must have discovered her problem! Please enjoy this half marshmallow!"

Jonah didn't know what made these marshmallows so good, but they were the best he'd ever eaten. Cheeks still full, Jonah turned to Garbo. "Do you know how to get to the forest?"

"As chance would have it, I do, my boy! Surely you must know that turkeys sleep in trees!" he answered, smiling wide. "Let me take some bark from this locust and draw a map for Miss Yeti in the dirt near that garden."

Garbo made his way quickly to the ground and sketched out a crude set of directions for the Yeti. As he was working, the Yeti climbed her way down the tree and across the grass.

Just as Garbo was finishing the map, the Yeti peered over his shoulder, which was no small feat since she was so tall and Garbo, in comparison, was so short.

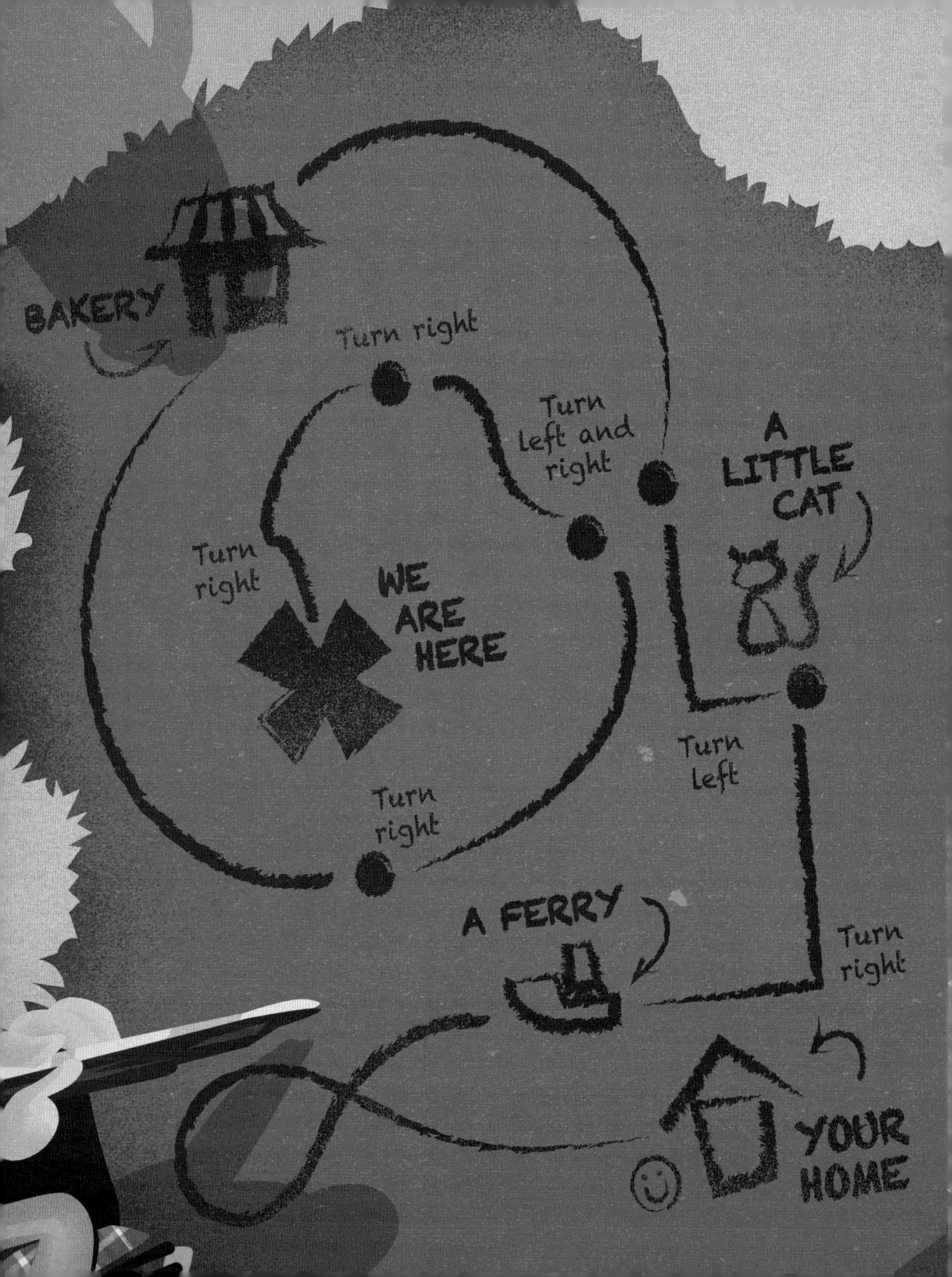
BAKERY
Turn right
Turn left and right
A LITTLE CAT
Turn right
WE ARE HERE
Turn left
Turn right
A FERRY
Turn right
YOUR HOME

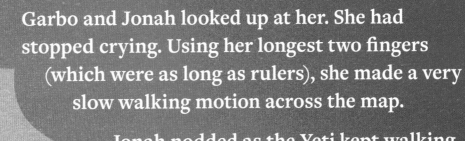

Garbo and Jonah looked up at her. She had stopped crying. Using her longest two fingers (which were as long as rulers), she made a very slow walking motion across the map.

Jonah nodded as the Yeti kept walking her fingers along the map. Suddenly, he knew what she was trying to tell them.

"It's going to take you a very long time to get home, isn't it?" Jonah asked. The Yeti nodded.

Garbo slipped Jonah another half marshmallow for his good detective work.

"Here, you can take my skateboard! You'll be home before dark if you ride this thing!"

The Yeti took the skateboard in her hands and turned it over, curiously. She handed it back to Jonah.

"No, really, you can do it," Jonah encouraged her. He walked over to the sidewalk and demonstrated how to use the skateboard before handing it back to her.

"Please take it, and get home safely," Jonah said.

The Yeti took the skateboard from Jonah and stood on top of it. She teetered a little bit, but seemed to gain her balance quickly. She then pushed off, one slow kick at a time, toward the end of the block. When she reached the intersection, she turned around and waved to Jonah and Garbo, a huge, footprint-sized smile stretched across her face. Then she kicked off and disappeared around the corner toward home.

Jonah's eyes grew wide. **"Garbo, we did it! We solved the mystery!"** he grinned.

"I believe you earned this for a job most well done, dear Jonah," Garbo said, handing Jonah the fifth and final marshmallow. Jonah chewed it eagerly as they walked back toward Jonah's house.

"Good day to you, my young detective," Garbo said, tipping his hat and vanishing from sight.

Now how am I going to get a new skateboard? Jonah wondered, closing his front door behind him.

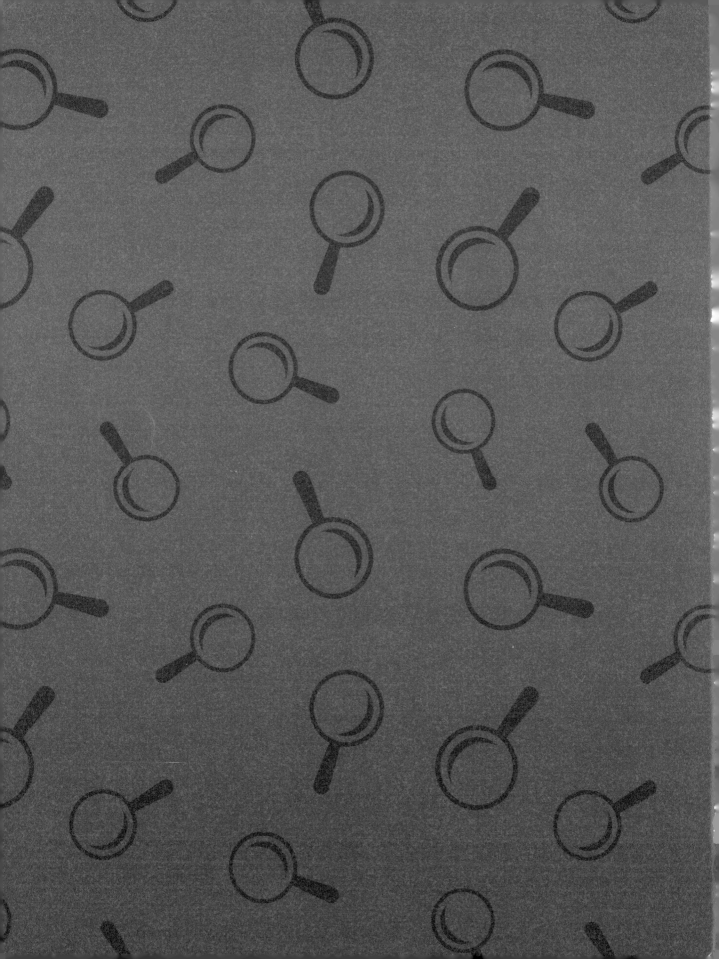